DATE DUE

Fart Squad #4: The Toilet Vortex
Text copyright © 2016 by Full Fathom Five, LLC
Illustrations copyright © 2016 by Full Fathom Five, LLC
All rights reserved. Printed in the United States of America. No part of this book may be used or repro-
duced in any manner whatsoever without written permission except in the case of brief quotations
embodied in critical articles and reviews. For information address HarperCollins Children's Books, a
division of HarperCollins Publishers, 195 Broadway, New York, NY 10007.
www.harpercollinschildrens.com

Library of Congress Control Number: 2015951375
ISBN 978-0-06-236634-4 (trade bdg.)—ISBN 978-0-06-229051-9 (pbk.)

Design by Victor Joseph Ochoa
16 17 18 19 20   CG/OPM   10 9 8 7 6 5 4 3 2 1
❖
First Edition

FART SQUAD

THE TOILET VORTEX

by **SEAMUS PILGER**

illustrated by **STEPHEN GILPIN**

JF
HM 4/97
4.99
8/18

HARPER
An Imprint of HarperCollins Publishers

full fathom five

CHAPTER ONE

"**I** think I'm going to be sick," Darren Stonkadopolis groaned as he backed away from the toilet.

Janitor Stan leaned over his shoulder to get a better look at the offending specimen. "Oh, you're fine," he said. "Happens all the time." And with the push of one finger, Stan flushed that toilet good.

Stan was the only human being whom Darren and his friends trusted to keep their identity as the elusive superhero team, the Fart Squad, a secret. He also doubled as their coach, or scent-sei. Cleaning up toilets after school wasn't exactly how Darren would have chosen to demonstrate his gratitude. But when Stan asked Darren for help with a running toilet, Darren just couldn't say no.

"Okay," Stan declared to the otherwise empty bathroom, "which one of you won't shut up?" He eyed the row of stalls before pointing to the far end. "Aha, gotcha!" he announced.

Darren followed the janitor to the last stall. "No water on the floor," Stan said as they stopped in front of it. "That's good." He pushed the stall door open, and Darren shivered. Suddenly it was really, really cold in there!

Stan grabbed the toilet handle and tried jiggling it. The water kept running, forming a swirling vortex in the center of the bowl. He lifted the lid off the toilet's tank and peered inside. "Everything looks okay," he told Darren, "but sometimes something gets knocked loose."
Then, much to Darren's horror, the janitor reached inside the toilet's tank and fiddled with a valve, but the water kept on running.

"Nothing there," Stan said, pulling his arm from the tank and drying it on a rag from his back pocket. "Could be something clogging the actual toilet pipe, I guess. What's weird is the toilets up here have been doing this all week—every time I get one to stop, another starts acting up." He studied the toilet bowl and the water swirling down into it before finally sticking his hand in there, as well, causing Darren to gag.

"There's definitely suction," he reported. "A whole lot of it, actually. In fact"—his shoulder twitched and wrenched, but his hand was still in the toilet—"I think I'm stuck!"

"What?" Darren grabbed the janitor's free hand and tried to pull him loose. It didn't help. Then the rushing-water noise got louder, and suddenly Stan jerked forward, his arm in as far down as his shoulder.

"There's definitely something wrong

with this toilet!" Stan said, bracing both feet against the toilet base and pulling with all his might. But he couldn't get his hand back out. And now more of his arm was being pulled down into the toilet! It was like the toilet was a monstrous mouth swallowing up the janitor!

"It's no use. I'm going down!" Stan shouted, struggling against the pull. Darren tried tugging him free again. Still no success.

There was a scuffling noise as Stan's feet left the ground, his shoulder and part of his chest in the toilet bowl now. Then, with a loud slurp, his head and upper body disappeared down the pipe, as well.

"No!" Darren cried, tugging on Stan's leg. A second later Darren lost his grip as Stan's legs went, and the toilet swallowed

the janitor completely. His wrench made a loud *clang* as it fell to the floor by the toilet, after which the bathroom was quiet except for the rush of running water. "Stan!" Darren shouted into the toilet.

"Help!" Stan shouted, sounding very far away.

"Stan!" Darren called again. But this time he got no answer.

"STAAAAAAAAAAAAAN!"

CHAPTER TWO

"**H**urry up!" Darren shouted as he waved Juan-Carlos Finkelstein toward him. "The toilet swallowed Stan. We've got to save him!"

"What do you mean, it swallowed him?" Juan-Carlos asked, running as fast as he could. As soon as he'd gotten over his shock at Stan's disappearance, Darren had texted the Squad to meet in front of the third-floor boys' bathroom.

When little Tina Heiney caught up with them she was just as confused. "How is that even possible?"

"I don't know," Darren replied. "We have superpowered farts. How is *that* possible?"

"He has a point," Walter Turnip declared, bringing up the rear and huffing to a stop. Bigger and heavier than the others, he wasn't exactly built for speed. "Given our own new abilities, and some of the strange things we have encountered since, we should keep an open mind."

They were an odd foursome—jittery

Darren, tiny Tina, lanky joker Juan-Carlos, and bulky brain Walter—but they had bonded when the school's mystery burritos had given each of them strange superpowers. Or superfarts, really. And that was how they'd become the Fart Squad.

"Okay, fine, a toilet swallowed him." Tina crossed her arms. "Grab a plunger and get him back out."

"It's way too late for that," Darren argued. "He got sucked in completely. It was like ... magic."

"So what do we do?" Juan-Carlos sighed. "This is normally when we'd ask Stan for advice!"

Darren nodded. Since forming the Fart Squad, Stan had really become a mentor to them all. How would the team function at all without the janitor's wisdom and common sense? Darren took a deep breath. "We're going to have to jump in after him."

"You want us to jump into a toilet?" Juan-Carlos shook his head. "Man, this Squad is really going down the drain!" As usual, nobody laughed at his awful joke.

"Let's go!" Tina said, fearless as always.

"Are you sure?" Juan-Carlos asked her. "You won't feel weird about going into the boy's bathroom?"

"Feelings?" Tina scoffed. "Who has time for feelings?" And with that, Tina walked herself right into the bathroom.

"Looks normal to me," she said, unimpressed. "Gross, but normal."

Walter followed Tina inside and then all four Squad members gathered around the toilet. Oddly, the water swirling in the bowl was a deep blue that almost seemed to glow. It was very pretty—hypnotic, almost.

Walter leaned in over the toilet bowl, studying the roiling water, then reached for the handle.

"Wait!" Darren shouted. He batted Walter's hand away. "Look, we don't know what'll happen if we do that. It could grab us, too. We don't know where it goes. We don't know anything except that it took Stan." He gulped. "We should probably think about it before making our next move."

Walter backed away. "Agreed." Then he brightened. "Time for a snack?" he asked.

The others knew that wasn't just Walter's

stomach speaking. What he meant was that it was time to eat some of the school's super-special burritos—the ones that gave them their powers.

"Yeah," Tina agreed. She glanced at the toilet again and shook her head. "Also, we need our Fart Squad uniforms. If we're really going to do this, let's do it right!"

A few minutes later, the farty foursome met back at Janitor Stan's closet dressed in uniform, looking every bit the heroes they'd become in the past several weeks.

Darren loaded up Stan's microwave, and three minutes later he pulled out a freshly warmed-over plate of bean burritos. "Come and get it!" he shouted.

"Bottoms up!" Juan-Carlos joked as Darren set the plate down in front of them. The others groaned but dug in. In record time the plate was wiped clean and the Fart Squad members were gassed up and ready to go!

Darren led the way back up to the bathroom and the end stall, where he and his friends stood around the toilet, staring at their futures.

"Is this truly our best course of action?" Walter asked. "To pursue our missing mentor into the very commode that stole him from us?"

"If anybody's got a better idea, let me know," Darren replied. He wasn't so sure himself. If only Stan were here! He'd know what to do!

But nobody had a better idea. And who else was going to help in a situation like this? This was exactly the sort of problem someone would call on the Fart Squad to handle—and they *were* the Fart Squad!

Darren studied the toilet. "One of us should go first and see what happens."

The others nodded. Then they all looked at one another. Finally Juan-Carlos clapped Darren on the back. "Good job volunteering!" he said.

Darren sighed. As leader of the Fart Squad, he often had to do things that scared him. Not to mention things that repulsed him. Besides, his power was superhot farts that burned his butt on their way out. How much worse could a toilet be? He tried not to think about that too hard.

"Fine. Just, I don't know, watch and listen in case I need help." He stepped up onto the toilet seat, the water swirling below him. "Here goes nothing!" Then he took a deep breath and closed his eyes, stepped off the seat, and plunged feetfirst into the toilet bowl.

Whoosh!

It was like being

sucked into a vacuum cleaner underwater. The toilet pulled Darren in, swirling him around at the same time, as if he were going down a water slide. And just like on a water slide, a few seconds later he splashed down, spluttering as his head went under.

"Blub, ack!" Darren gasped, swallowing some water and choking a little before he found his feet and stood up. He was submerged up to his waist.

"Oh gross," he muttered, raising his arms and shaking them. Not that it helped any. He was soaked from head to toe.

Darren looked around, and immediately he wished he hadn't.

Water seeping into his boots and making his clothes stick to him, and the smell—oh man, the smell!—told him he was definitely not in Kansas anymore.

"So," Darren muttered to himself, trying to keep it together, "this is what a sewer looks like."

It was pretty disgusting. A giant tunnel with grimy tiled walls that curved up on both sides splattered with yellow and brown streaks.

And chunks.

Smaller tunnels branched off to the sides here and there. Bare lightbulbs were strung up overhead, just enough to cast a lot of gloomy shadows.

There were *things* floating in the water, too—small, dark things; large, lumpy things.

Darren really didn't want to examine those too closely. And then, of course, the kernels of corn. As bright and yellow and pristine as if they were freshly shucked off the cob.

Corn, Darren thought.

The indestructible cockroaches of the human digestive system.

As Darren tried to find his footing in the slippery slop of stinky waste, something small and green bumped up against him, and Darren automatically reached out and grabbed it. It was a small toy soldier. The little plastic figure's rifle had snapped off and his helmet looked like someone had chewed on it.

"Odd," Darren muttered.

The other thing out of place here—besides Darren himself—was the glowing blue portal hovering beside him just above the water. It was exactly the same color as the toilet bowl, and so cold, just being near it was making his teeth chatter.

"Hey, guys, can you hear me?" he shouted into the portal. "I'm okay! Seriously grossed out, but okay!" He looked around again. "I don't see Stan anywhere, though!"

"I don't know who Stan is," a voice answered, "but I hope you like the sewers, 'cause you're here to stay!" The voice wasn't coming from the portal, though. It was coming from behind him!

Darren whipped around. A man, wrapped in toilet paper like a mummy, was floating toward him from a side tunnel. Three other figures emerged from the same tunnel and joined the man. The four TP-wrapped men quickly surrounded Darren.

"Uh-oh," he muttered. "This is a whole new level of deep doo-doo."

CHAPTER THREE

"**G**eronimo!" a familiar voice sounded. Shadows enveloped Darren. He glanced back and saw that a patch of darkness had blotted out most of the light coming from the portal beside him.

The next thing Darren knew, a large form shot out into the sewer, slamming straight into the men and bowling them over into the water. It was Walter!

"We decided it would be better to face whatever was down here together," Darren's friend told him as he clambered back to his feet, shaking droplets everywhere. "We are a team, after all."

"Exactly," Tina agreed, appearing out of the portal and plummeting into the water with a splash, but managing to land on her feet. One of the TP mummies made the mistake of trying to grab her, and despite being immersed up to her elbows she kicked him in the shins and sent him howling into the shadows.

"Back off!" she warned.

Juan-Carlos arrived last. "Just bringing up the rear," he said, slapping his butt—and now it was four against four.

"Holy crap," Juan-Carlos added, gagging. "This really is gross!" He frantically waved his hands, trying to flick off whatever had stuck to them.

"I think I've got poop on my hands!" he shrieked.

Walter nodded in agreement. "Indeed, your metacarpus appears to be smeared with fresh excrement." He took a closer look. "And judging by the greenish hue, whosoever emitted this particular nugget is woefully due for a visit to their trusted internal-medicine professional."

Just then a stern voice bellowed, "You kids are in big trouble." A TP man sneered. He and his comrades were big, Darren realized. As big around the middle as Walter, but taller. They moved smoothly through the water, almost as if they were swimming instead of walking, but their arms waved about aimlessly, as did the tufts of hair poking up from the wrappings on top of their heads.

"Give up and come quietly and we won't hurt you."

"Hurt *us*?" Tina laughed despite the stains now coating her uniform. "*You* give up and *we* won't hurt *you*!"

The men paused for a second. They obviously weren't used to people standing up to them, especially not tiny little girls.

Darren could see Tina was ready to fight, as always. But what they really needed were answers. "Where's Stan the Janitor?" he demanded.

"Who's Stan the Janitor?" one of the men asked.

"Our scent-sei," Tina snapped. "You kidnapped him!"

"No idea," one soldier answered. "But you've got bigger problems right now."

He and his friends surged in closer.

Darren sighed. Clearly they weren't going to get any answers here. "Fine," he said. "Let 'em have it, gang!"

"You got it, chief!" Juan-Carlos answered. He closed his eyes and grimaced as he released a time-bomb fart, then tried to run away. But the water wasn't letting him get very far, very fast.

"Uh, misfire here," he called out. A few bubbles floated to the surface behind him. If they smelled at all, nobody could tell in the general sewer stink.

"I, too, am experiencing mishaps of a technical variety," Walter agreed. He was straining upward as hard as he could, but aside from a little bobbing, he couldn't get any momentum. "It appears the water and the cold are hampering my abilities."

Darren glanced at Tina, who shrugged. "I got nothing," she agreed.

"Guess it's up to me," Darren muttered. Turning, he presented his backside to the approaching men. Then he concentrated.

Fssssssssss!

It was useless. The water level was above their butts, absorbing their gaseous emissions and fizzling them into nothingness.

The TP man in front cackled like Count Dracula. "Mwah-ha-ha! Are you all done trying to 'get us'? Because now it's our turn!"

For someone who was completely wrapped in toilet paper, this soldier did a heck of a job being scary.

"Uh, on second thought," Darren said, raising both hands, "we give up."

His friends looked shocked, but quickly surrendered, as well. Without their powers, they were just kids, after all. Against four big, scary guys, they didn't stand a chance. Especially without their scent-sei there to tell them what to do next!

"We'll take these prisoners to the Head for questioning," the man in front told the others.

As they led the kids away, Darren couldn't help but wonder where Stan was. And whether they'd ever find him—or, without their powers, ever get out of here at all.

He shuddered.

Was the Fart Squad doomed to the bottom of the bowl forever?

CHAPTER FOUR

"This place is disgusting," Juan-Carlos whined as he picked his way past mounds of something they couldn't easily identify and really didn't want to.

"Oh, suck it up," Tina told him. Despite being the only girl, she was easily the toughest member of the Squad.

"Indeed," Walter offered, "the terrain, the odor, and the contents of this water are all consistent with what one would expect from a functioning waste disposal system." He wrinkled his nose in distaste. "And while certain African tribes still fashion their huts out of dried cow dung, wading through moist human . . . well, how should I say—I seem to be running out of synonyms—*dookie*, is an entirely different story both physically and psychologically."

Walter glanced up at the curving ceiling high overhead, no doubt thinking how much easier it would be to just fly away from these men—and all this sewage—and search for Stan from high above, in flight, propelled by the jet stream produced by his all-powerful farts.

They waded through tunnels for what felt like hours until Tina broke the silence. "Really?" she asked, when she spotted a large white egg shape on the horizon. "*That's* your headquarters?"

But when the four friends stood at the base of the imposing structure, there was no

question it was the Head. It was a large dome, easily twenty feet high, and it appeared to be made entirely of smooth, gleaming white porcelain. In short, it was a giant toilet bowl turned upside down and planted in the middle of the sewer.

"Well, you wouldn't have any trouble finding it in the dark," Juan-Carlos joked.

"Inside," one of the soldiers commanded. He led the way to a wide, round opening. Two more wrapped men blocked the way. "Prisoners," he told them, and they nodded, stepping aside so the group could enter.

Darren had the feeling the TP creatures wouldn't be letting him and his friends back out so easily.

The dome's interior was just as clean and white as the exterior. Darren had worried that it would be dark, since he hadn't seen any windows, but discovered he could see just fine. He glanced up and saw that the top of the dome was a big round opening, like a skylight but without any glass. Extra lights had been strung around it to reflect off the shiny white walls.

Not that there was much to see. There weren't any inside walls—just the one big circular room—and the floor was covered with water, like a large, shallow pool. At least the water wasn't high, Darren thought. In here it was only up to his ankles.

The guards led them straight across, toward the far end. As the kids approached, they saw a massive chair, made of white ceramic like the building itself, with a high back and thick arms. A man sat there, leaning back and watching them. He was short and stubby, and wrapped in toilet paper like his men. Only his big round eyes and a single spike of wispy red-gold hair right on top showed through. In his chubby hands he held what looked like a staff, and a shiny white crown sat atop his head.

"And what's this?" he asked as they stopped just before him. "Children? We don't get those down here! Did someone flush you?" He laughed like that was a big joke. "Perhaps they mistook you for waste?" The guards found that particular joke to be the funniest of all.

"Kneel!" One of the soldiers demanded, shoving Darren to the floor. "Kneel before the Porcelain Throne. Kneel before the Royal Flush, king of the sewer!"

They knelt, trying not to squirm in disgust at the sewer water.

"You people flush the funniest things," the Royal Flush continued. "Toilet paper, of course. Food—eaten and otherwise. Sometimes jewelry or keys, though I'm guessing those are accidents. Plenty of toys. Even some living things. Small creatures of the sea. He leaned forward, studying the foursome closely. "But never people." He stroked his chin. "How did you find your way down to my soggy little kingdom?"

"You took our friend!" Darren answered.

"Yeah, where's Stan?" Tina chimed in.

"Stan? Ah, yes." The Royal Flush leaned back in his chair, sounding very pleased with himself. "He was messing up my plans, fixing those toilets. I couldn't have that, so I dragged him down here instead."

"Where is he?" Juan-Carlos asked.

"You better not have hurt him!" Walter added.

"You're so concerned about him," the king replied, waving his hand. "You'd be better off worrying about yourselves."

Darren gulped and looked around, noticing just how bad this was. No Stan in sight, no powers, and a bunch of scary guys in toilet paper all around. "Uh, we just came to get our friend," he said, shivering a little. "If you tell us where he is, we'll take him and go. He won't cause any more trouble, I promise."

"Somehow I don't think I can trust you," the Royal Flush told them. "So instead I'll just keep you. Forever." He smiled through his toilet-paper wrappings. "But don't worry, you'll soon have lots of company."

"What's that supposed to mean?" Tina demanded. Darren had a feeling if the guards weren't holding them back, she'd have kicked the king in the shins by now.

"It means, little girl," the Royal Flush answered, "that your kind have been flushing all sorts of waste down here for as long as anyone can remember." He plucked a broken toy car from the water near his throne and flung it at them. "I'm done with all that. This time I intend to flush back! I have been opening portals into your world, but each time I do, your friend comes along and closes them! Well, not this time! Now the portal is *all ours*! Soon it will grow wide enough for my army to fit through. Then we will conquer the world up above!"

He started waving his plunger scepter around, and the nearby guards and soldiers all shouted and cheered. "We will finally

get to live in sunlight and warmth, with dry land and flowers and all sorts of nice, clean things. And you"—he leaned forward and pointed his plunger at them—"you and all of your kind can waste away down here in the dark, cold, smelly old sewers, with all the poop you put here in the first place!"

CHAPTER FIVE

"**Y**ou can't do that!" Darren shouted, trying to charge at the Royal Flush. But the TP men held him back. *If only I could use my fart power,* Darren thought. But he was still too soggy. They all were.

"Oh?" The king glared down at him. "And why not? Who's going to stop me? Your friend? He'll have a ringside seat! Or you? A handful of annoying kids?" He laughed again, and so did all of his guards. Then he stopped and the room fell silent.

"Throw them in the tank," the Royal Flush

commanded. "They can wait there for all the rest of their kind!"

The guards grabbed the kids by the arms and started to haul them away. Darren tried farting again out of desperation, but produced only a few bubbles and some steam. He was just too waterlogged to do anything! So were the rest of the Squad. Tina struggled,

but the guards just laughed as they dragged her across the floor. There had to be something they could do!

The guards brought the foursome up a short flight of steps to a small platform behind the throne. Facing the platform was a single doorway, round like the one into the Head itself. The door opened onto a narrow

hall that led
down into the
ground. Darren
peered inside,
but it was too dark
to see where the hall-
way led.

"Down," one of the
guards instructed, leading the
way. These guys really didn't talk
much!

The hallway led to a single large, rectan-
gular room well below the Head. The walls
and floor and ceiling here were the same
white porcelain all around. And more important, because the door had been up higher,
no water had ever made its way in here, so
the place was dry.

The guards pulled out glow sticks so they
could see where they were going and led the

kids down to the bottom. Darren suddenly realized with a shock that when the Royal Flush had said "Throw them in the tank," he had meant exactly that—the Head was an upside-down toilet, and the area they were in right now was the attached water tank!

The guards shoved the Squad into one of the cells in the back of the tank, then closed the door with a loud clang and locked it up tight.

"Enjoy your stay," one of them said. He and the other guards walked away, laughing. They took their lights with them. There was one glow stick mounted high up along the wall at the back of the cell, but it barely provided enough light for the Squad to see one another.

"What now, oh fearless leader?" Walter asked, once they'd heard the guards stomp back up the stairs. "We still have no idea where Stan might be, and now we're imprisoned, too."

Darren tried to imagine what their scentsei would say in this situation and smiled slowly as it came to him. "What now?" he answered. "We fight back! We're the Fart Squad!" He shook himself off, spraying water everywhere like a great, big dog.

"Hey, quit it!" Tina demanded.

"No, he is correct," Walter said. He smiled. "We all need to dry out as quickly

as possible." He shook himself, as well, and Tina and Juan-Carlos followed. After a few minutes the kids were almost dry.

"Good enough?" Tina asked.

"One way to find out," Darren replied. He turned around, aimed his butt at the door, and finally released the fart he'd been holding back since they'd reached the Head.

Blatttttt!

The fiery flatulence shot across the gap between him and the stall door like a flaming spear. The door melted away from the heat, leaving a wide opening. The heat

also evaporated the rest of the water off him and the others. Now they were all dry again and ready for action!

Darren stepped out of the stall, feeling a lot surer of himself now that he and his co-Squad members had their powers back. "That'll bring those guards running. Better get ready!"

"I'm on it," Juan-Carlos called out, ducking away toward the exit. He returned a minute later. The Squad could already hear the sound of heavy footsteps descending. It was the guards. They had obviously heard the noise, but were still out of sight when there was a loud wheezing sound and a horrific smell, followed by choking and gasping noises. Juan-Carlos's time-bomb fart had gone off perfectly!

"Got 'em!" Juan-Carlos cheered.

The guards stumbled into view, still

dazed from the fart. There were three of them, and they all staggered toward the cell, but stopped when they saw the melted door.

"What the crap?!" One of them shouted as they all raised their plungers, ready to attack.

"Oh, please don't hurt me!" Tina cried, throwing up her hands. The guards surrounded her, but it was clear they didn't consider her a threat. That was their big

mistake. A second later, two of them stiffened, gulped, and collapsed. Tina's silent-but-deadly farts had knocked them out cold. "You messed with the wrong kids," she said with a smile.

That just left the one guard. He tried backing away toward the stairs, but Walter floated up and leapfrogged over him, blocking his exit. Then he knocked the man out cold with a karate kick, and the soldier crumpled to the ground.

"Now can we get out of here?" Juan-Carlos asked.

But Darren shook his head. "We still need to find Stan," Darren reminded his friends. "Besides, the Royal Flush is going to invade our world and take it over! We've got to stop him!" It was what Stan would tell them to do, no doubt.

"We are our world's only defense against a veritable legion of poop," Walter agreed. Then he chuckled. "May the best bodily function win!"

Juan-Carlos and Tina nodded. "Let's go, then," she told Darren.

The Fart Squad began their escape, first climbing up the narrow hallway and from there out into the Royal Flush's immense throne room. Darren had worried about having to fight their way past a whole bunch of guards, but it turned out he didn't have to fret. The throne room was complete empty!

"Uh-oh," Tina said. "That's a bad sign."

"Hurry!" Darren took the lead, sprinting down the steps and wading across the pool. His friends raced along behind him. He slowed when they reached the exit, afraid there would still be soldiers stationed outside, but those posts were empty, as well. "He's taken every last soldier with him," Darren muttered. "That means they must be ready to go! We can't let them pass through that portal!"

"How will we locate them?" Walter asked. "I confess to having gotten completely disoriented on our journey here."

Surprisingly, Juan-Carlos smiled. "Follow the cold," he answered, and after a second the others nodded. Of course! The portal was freezing cold and made the water cold around it. The farther they'd gotten from there, the warmer the water had become. So if they headed toward colder water, it should lead them back to the portal!

"This time, however, there is no need to slog through filth," Walter declared. He grabbed Juan-Carlos with one hand and Darren with the other, then grimaced and let out a series of small, squeaky farts. Darren quickly caught Tina's hand with his free one as they all lifted off the ground. Whew! The smell of the sewer still overwhelmed them, but at least they weren't walking through it this time!

Walter flew them down the tunnels. Each time he came to a turn, he went whichever way felt coldest. Finally they found themselves at the end of one tunnel, peeking out at a much wider one ahead—and at a glowing blue disc of light, hovering just above the water, maybe a hundred feet ahead of them. It was the portal. Darren almost cheered at the sight of it. Just a single step would take them all home.

Unfortunately, they still didn't know where Stan was, and standing between them and the portal were hundreds upon hundreds of soldiers.

And unless Darren could think of something quick, poor, unsuspecting Buttzville was about to be invaded by the Royal Flush.

CHAPTER SIX

"We've got to get through that portal and warn everyone!" Tina insisted. They had ducked back down the side tunnel and Walter had found a narrow ledge to land upon. This way he didn't have to carry them but they could still stay dry enough to use their powers.

"Yeah, but how?" Juan-Carlos asked.

"We've got another problem," Tina added. She gestured back around the corner. "See that?" A large white tent floated upon the disgusting sewer water, perhaps forty feet from the portal. "What do you want to bet that's where the Royal Flush is? And remember what he said about Stan? He'd have a ringside seat."

The others gasped. Of course! The Royal Flush didn't want Stan interfering, so the king was keeping him close by. They'd found him! But how were they going to get to him there, surrounded by the enemy?

"We need a distraction," Walter suggested. "Something to draw them away while we rescue Stan."

"A distraction?" *What would Stan do?* Darren wondered. *What would Stan do?*

"If only Stan were around to help Darren plot out Stan's rescue!" Juan-Carlos quipped. It was almost as if he were reading Darren's mind.

"Juan-Carlos," Darren said after a second, "can you set one of your farts right where the two tunnels meet?"

"Absolutely. When do you want it to go off?"

Darren thought about it. "Wait until I do my thing, then give me a minute." Next he turned to Tina and Walter. "Once I distract them, you go get Stan. There may be some soldiers left, so you'll have to knock them out."

Tina grinned. "Not a problem."

"As soon as I leave, get ready," Darren told the others. "Once it all hits the fan, we'll only have a few seconds to reach the portal." *And we'll probably only have a few more seconds in the water before we're too soaked and frozen to do anything,* he thought.

"Good luck," Tina told Darren as he prepared to slip away.

"Thanks." Then Darren turned and headed back the way they'd come. He stuck to the ledge until he spotted a big mound of poo floating right in the middle of the water. Trying not to breathe in the smell, he turned around and bent over so his butt was angled toward the mound.

And then he let it rip.

Blattttttttttt!

A stream of stinky fire shot from his rear—and lit the poo on fire. Within seconds the entire mound was burning. Thick black smoke billowed up from it. The smell was so bad Darren almost gagged, but he didn't have time to be sick. Instead he ran back down the tunnel, toward the portal.

"Fire!" he shouted. "The sewer is on fire!"

CHAPTER SEVEN

Darren raced back toward the portal. He saw Juan-Carlos waiting by the entrance to the main tunnel. Juan-Carlos gave him a thumbs-up.

Then the soldiers came spilling around the corner. They all froze, staring at the burning pile of poo ahead.

And that's when Juan-Carlos's time-bomb fart went off around them. The men disappeared into a cloud of stink and fell back, gasping.

Bull's-eye!

"Now!" Darren shouted as he reached his teammate. "Let's go!"

They turned and raced around the corner toward the portal, jumping into the water to splash across. There were a few soldiers still by the tent, but as Darren watched, a large figure barreled through them and the men collapsed as he passed. Walter!

Right behind him, wading through the

sewer water, was a familiar stocky gray-haired man.

Tina darted out of the tent behind him.

Tina spotted Darren and Juan-Carlos and waved. "It was perfect," she shouted as they approached. "Walter carried me over the water and I wiped them all out!"

Darren nodded. "Are you okay?" he asked Stan.

The janitor nodded. "I'm fine," he answered. "But I don't think we should stick around here much longer."

Behind them, they could hear the soldiers recovering from Juan-Carlos's attack. It was too late, though. The Squad had reached the portal. Darren got there first and, in typical Darren fashion, jumped straight in.

It was just like when he'd gotten sucked in, only in reverse. His whole world seemed to swirl around him, spinning and tugging him. Then he found himself shooting out of the toilet bowl.

Whoosh!

Darren landed hard on his butt just outside the last stall of the boys' room. Right back where they'd started.

"Ouch," he muttered, rubbing his sore bottom. Between his fiery farts and falling and running into things, his butt was getting a lot of abuse these days.

"Look out below!" a voice called from the vicinity of the toilet. Darren scrambled to his feet. He managed to get out of the way just before Juan-Carlos came crashing through, landing in almost the exact same spot. Darren grabbed his friend by the shoulder and dragged him to the side before any of the others could come through. "Careful," he warned. The floor was covered in water, making it super slippery, and the toilet was still overflowing. They both clutched on to the sinks opposite the stalls, trying not to fall again.

Darren held on, trying to steady himself. Then something moved nearby. Darren looked up and realized they weren't alone in the bathroom.

"Attack!" a soldier standing by the door shouted. He and two others charged at Darren and Juan-Carlos, waving their heavy plungers.

"Whoa, back up, dude!" Juan-Carlos yelped. "Do I look like a clogged drain to

you?" He ducked around the soldiers, and a
moment later one of his stinky time bombs
went off right where he'd been standing. The
soldiers paused their headlong rush, shaking their heads side to side, eyes watering.
But they kept coming.

"Clear the way, coming through!" Walter

announced an instant before he arrived outside the stall, breathing hard. He hadn't slipped like Darren and Juan-Carlos had because he was still floating a few inches off the ground. "Well, that was certainly—oh my, what have we here?" He'd spotted the soldiers.

"Don't worry, I've got this one," Darren assured him. Turning around and bracing himself against the sink, he let loose a stream of fart-fire that stopped the men dead in their tracks. They scuttled away from the

stinky heat, waving their arms to put out the fire licking at their wrappings.

"Nice work!" Stan said, having just appeared. Tina was with him.

"Quiet! Listen!" she told the others.

They all did as she said, stopping and listening—and right away they heard the stomping of many heavy feet. It was coming from out in the hall.

"There are more of them out there!" Tina announced.

"We need to stop them before those soldiers find their way out of the school building and hurt somebody!" Darren said. The others nodded. "Come on, Fart Squad, let's save some lives!"

They pushed past the three cowering soldiers, out into the hall. Fortunately, it was after school, so there weren't any teachers or other students around. But the hall was still

full—of TP soldiers! They all turned when they heard the bathroom door open, and the kids found themselves staring up at a mob of large, angry-looking figures wrapped in toilet paper.

"It's those kids!" one of the soldiers shouted. "Get them!"

Stan eyed the mess. There were puddles of dirty water and crumpled garbage and scraps of used toilet paper everywhere.

"Well, this is going to take a while to clean up," he said, shaking his head. "But I'll worry about that after." He grabbed his mop and swung it at a pair of soldiers, knocking them on their butts.

Walter nodded and ducked into a nearby classroom, returning a few seconds later carrying a flagpole. "I will strike from above!" he declared, a strong, sustained fart lifting him six feet into the air. Several shorter farts propelled him forward, the flagpole slamming into the soldiers' heads as Walter flew past, knocking them off their feet.

"Nice one, Walter!" Juan-Carlos cheered. He ran after his friend, stopping for a moment next to each downed soldier. A few seconds later, his farts erupted, knocking the men down just as they got back to their feet.

Tina went next, and a wave of her silent-but-deadly farts soon filled the hall with a powerful odor that left the soldiers unconscious.

Darren came last, using his fart-fire to drive away any men trying to hit his friends. Stan was right beside him, shoving the soldiers away with his mop. Between them, they managed to herd all of the remaining invaders back into the bathroom.

"That's all of them for now," Darren said once they were all gathered again outside the bathroom door. "But you know the Royal Flush is going to send more of them through any second. What're we going to do then?"

"We need to find a way to shut that toilet down!" Tina declared. The others agreed.

"Any ideas?" Darren asked.

CHAPTER EIGHT

"**O**h, I do!" Juan-Carlos announced. The others groaned, expecting another lame joke, but this time their friend was serious. "That toilet's overflowing now, right?" he said. "And the Royal Flush changed the portal so it's spitting his people out into our world instead of the other way around. Maybe if we can get it to flush again, it'll switch back to pulling people in, and we can send them all home!"

"Nice!" Darren agreed. "Stan, can you work your magic?"

"Absolutely!" the janitor agreed.

The five of them stormed back into the bathroom—and froze.

Standing there just outside the stall was the Royal Flush himself!

"You!" he shouted when he saw them. "This is all your fault!" He waved his scepter at them. "You tried to cook me alive!" Darren saw that the king's toilet paper was singed black here and there. It was also slipping in places, exposing what looked like

gold scales underneath.

"You're trying to take over the world!" Tina yelled back. "You deserve to be cooked!"

"Or flushed!" Juan-Carlos added.

The Royal Flush glared at him, his big eyes narrowing. "Never again!" he declared, taking a step toward the Squad. "This time I'm here to stay!"

"This time?" Darren stared at the king.

"What do you mean? You've been here before?"

"I was born here," the king snarled, inching forward some more. "And I was happy! Until I was flushed down the toilet!" He scowled, the spike on top of his head waving. "I almost died! Fortunately, there was magic in the sewer—the same magic I used to create the portal. It healed me, made me bigger, stronger. I found a new life there. But you humans kept raining poo and pee down on us!"

"Humans?" Walter asked, peering around Darren. "You say that as if you are not one of us." Then he gasped. "You are not, are you?"

"No!" The Royal Flush grabbed at his wrappings and tugged, the flimsy burnt toilet paper tearing away. "I'm not!"

Darren stared. So did his friends. Standing in front of them—was a goldfish.

A really, really big goldfish.

That explained the spike of hair, Darren thought. It was actually a fin. The two side fins were arms, and the tail had grown thick and strong and split apart to form legs.

It was like the goldfish had become a fish-man.

A really angry one.

"That's why you want to take over the world!" Darren realized. "To get revenge! On your owner, and all the other owners like them."

"They thought I was dead," the Royal Flush agreed, shaking loose the last scraps of paper. "Or they were just tired of me. I don't know. But they wanted me gone. So they flushed me. Just like my men." He gestured at the soldiers passed out by the sinks. "All of us, fish that were flushed away. The magic of the sewers made them big and strong, just like me." That was why they moved so easily through the water, Darren realized. The TP soldiers were actually fish-men!

The king was still talking, though. "We were all thrown away, left to rot down there." He sniffed. Then he scowled. "Well, now it's your turn!"

"I don't think so." The voice came from behind the king, and he turned. Somehow, Tina had snuck past him while he'd been talking. Now she smiled up at the big goldfish.

And the Royal Flush fell to the floor, gills fluttering as Tina's fart overpowered him.

"Hurry!" she told the others. "I don't know how well it works on fish!"

CHAPTER NINE

"You hold them back!" Stan announced. "I'll deal with the toilet!" He slipped and slid his way across the wet floor, past the unconscious Royal Flush, and to the stall.

The rest of the Squad was right behind him. Stan's heavy wrench was still on the floor next to the toilet, right where he'd dropped it. Now he grabbed it and got to work.

"You heard the scent-sei," Darren told his teammates. "Keep those soldiers down!" He fired off a fart at a soldier who'd woken up and was reaching for his plunger. The soldier yelped and ducked away.

Juan-Carlos ducked back out through the bathroom door. A second later he returned. "We've got more soldiers headed this way," he reported. There was a muffled burst outside, and the sounds of coughing. He grinned. "But not anymore." Obviously another one of his time bombs had gone off out there.

Two other soldiers had gotten back to their feet and were trying to charge past the Squad and the sinks to rescue their fallen leader. Walter floated up toward the ceiling, hovering over the others' heads, and used Stan's mop to push the men back.

Then Tina was next to them. The soldiers dropped once more.

"Got it!" Stan called out. The sound of rushing water ended as the toilet bowl finally stopped filling. He stood up, backed away, and jiggled the toilet handle.

Flush!

Stan quickly hopped out of the stall and ushered the kids to the far side of the room as the toilet began working properly again. The portal immediately started sucking the nearest soldiers back down to the sewers.

"No!" the Royal Flush shouted. He had woken up and was flopping about on the floor outside the stall, trying to push himself to his tail-feet with his fins. But it was no use. The portal had him. "This isn't over!" he shouted as he was sucked back into the swirling water. "I will have my revenge!"

Then he was gone. His crown and scepter were swept away with him.

"Quick, get them all over there!" Darren

told the others. They began using their farts and Stan's mop to force soldiers into the stall. Walter went out into the hall and began airlifting those soldiers who were still unconscious. Tina contented herself with kicking and shoving, since her farts would only knock them out again.

It took a few minutes, but finally all of the soldiers had been flushed back to their own world. The bathroom was empty except for Stan, the Squad, and a lot of water.

The toilet finally stopped, and the bathroom was filled with a welcome silence.

"We need to make sure this toilet never runs again," Tina pointed out.

"I can take care of that," Darren replied. He turned and aimed his butt at the toilet, or more precisely at the spot where it met the wall. "Fire in the hole!" He released a short, sharp fart, the stench wafting over them as the flames burst forth from his backside. It hit the place where the water pipe ran into the toilet, and melted right through it. "Done!"

It was true. With the pipe melted, the toilet would never be able to fill and flush again. Problem solved.

"I think I would have just turned off the water," Stan commented, "but this way is a lot more permanent." He grinned at them. "Thanks for coming to get me, kids!"

"Of course," Darren replied. "We couldn't let our scent-sei down!"

"What if they open more portals?" Juan-Carlos asked. "Won't they just try to come through again?"

Stan rubbed his chin. "I'll keep my eyes open," he promised. "In the meantime, I'll make sure the toilets here at school all work properly. As long as they don't turn into portals, that guy shouldn't be able to bother us again."

"Maybe we can find a way to help him clean up the sewers, or at least part of them," Darren suggested. "It is seriously disgusting down there."

Tina nodded. "If anybody could help, it'd be us," she agreed. Then she looked around. "Which is why—I'm out of here!"

"Go ahead on home," Stan agreed. "I've got this." He smiled at the Squad. "Thanks again."

"No problem," Darren told him.

"Yeah, yeah, you're welcome," Tina grumbled. "Can we go now?"

"She's right," Juan-Carlos joked. "Time to quit stalling."

The others all groaned as they left the bathroom. All except Stan, who grabbed his mop and bucket and started cleaning. Finally things in Buttzville were back to normal again.

For now, anyway.

THE END

Read a Sneak Peek of Book Five,
Fart Squad: Underpantsed!

CHAPTER ONE

Juan-Carlos Finkelstein was already late for school when the harsh reality of an empty dresser drawer stopped him in his tracks. "Mom!" he shrieked. "Where's my clean underwear?"

"I just bought a whole new bunch!" his mom called from downstairs. "Stop going through underwear so quickly!"

You have no idea, Juan-Carlos thought as he closed the empty drawer. That's when he noticed a pungent fartlike odor that wafted over his dresser. He was pretty sure he hadn't farted all morning, and besides, he didn't recognize the smell as his brand. But he had more important things to concentrate on at the moment, anyway, namely getting to school on time. So he turned his attention to his laundry hamper in the hopes of scrounging up a decent pair of boxers. When you're a superhero whose power comes from your superpowered farts, it tends to take a toll on your underwear collection.

A familiar voice from his clock radio made him pause. "Can you believe those kids?" a man asked. "Running around in masks, farting on everyone—I've heard of loving the smell of your *own* farts, but, these kids must think other people love the smell, as well!"

Juan-Carlos's father was a radio personality. He had his own morning show,

"Shockin' Sheckey," which he recorded live in his home studio, right in the Finkelstein basement. People either loved him or hated him—*or,* loved to hate him. Juan-Carlos, of course, thought his dad was a comedic genius. Even if he was picking on the Fart Squad right now.

His dad continued, "But seriously, folks, I'm just playing around. I actually think those kids are great! They really saved our butts—ha-ha!—with that whole itching thing, and again with that dinosaur, and who knows what else. They're stinking up the town—in the best possible way!"

Dad's a fan! Juan-Carlos thought happily. *Too bad I can't tell him that his son is one of those kids he's cheering for! Well, maybe someday.*

In the meantime, there was school to worry about. And that required clean clothes.

Pulling open the hamper, Juan-Carlos found two pairs of jeans, three T-shirts, five mismatched socks, and what looked like one of his dad's Grillmaster aprons. But no underwear.

Oh well. Mom must have already grabbed them, Juan-Carlos thought, peeling back the waistband of his pajama bottoms. "I'll have to wear these a second time."

Only when he looked down, there was nothing between his pajama bottoms and himself.

"I'm sure I was wearing them when I went to bed," he muttered under his breath. "Maybe they came off during my sleep somehow?"

He wanted to ask his mother—maybe she'd taken them? But that didn't make any sense. Besides, even if she had, it wasn't like he could yell at her for doing his laundry.

He'd just have to manage. She'd probably have a whole pile of clean underwear waiting when he got home.

By the time Juan-Carlos's bus arrived at school, he was in agony. Without underwear to provide a protective layer, his jeans were rubbing him raw! He had to move really slowly as he stepped off the bus and carefully made his way up the stairs and into the building. All around him, everyone seemed to be in slow motion, moving in the same cautious, pained manner he was.

When he finally reached his classroom, Juan-Carlos gratefully slid into his assigned seat. Now that he was sitting down, he noticed that his classmates were also moving slowly. *They all look exactly how I feel,*

Juan-Carlos thought. But there was no way his mom was washing all of *their* underwear, was there?

Clearly something else was going on here.

At lunchtime, Juan-Carlos sought out his friends. They were all wincing every time they shifted in their seats.

"Let me guess," tiny Tina Heiney said as she looked around the table. "No underwear, right?"

"Nothing," Juan-Carlos admitted. "Even the dirty pair from last night is gone. And I don't know about you guys, but there was an awful fart smell that most definitely did not come from me!"

"Same here!" Tina exclaimed. "Nothing

like smelling other people's farts first thing in the morning to ruin your day." Tina might have had a dainty appearance, but she talked like a truck driver.

"And do you guys believe that my mom actually accused me of throwing my underwear in the garbage!" Darren said.

The other three all nodded as if on cue.

"Indeed," said Walter.

"Pretty much!" Tina answered.

"Sounds about right," said Juan-Carlos.

"I guess you guys are right," Darren said, with a sigh.

The truth is throwing underwear in the garbage after one use is exactly the kind of thing Darren would do. He often acted without thinking, which got him in trouble at school, but made him the kind of quick-on-his-feet leader a team of superheroes like the Fart Squad needed.

"Apparently the problem is widespread. Your father referenced the undergarment situation this morning during his broadcast," Walter commented to Juan-Carlos. "He joked that all of Buttzville had been drafted into special forces, because we're all 'going commando,'" Walter continued. When the others stared at him blankly, Walter explained, "Going commando means *going it alone*. As in, getting dressed without putting on any underwear." Walter was as brainy as he was wide. He spent half the time explaining things to the rest of the Squad, and the other half of the time acting as their private blimp.

Tina rolled her eyes. "Guess we know where Juan-Carlos gets his sense of humor," she muttered.

Juan-Carlos brightened. "Really? Thanks!" That just made Tina roll her eyes again.

"It does seem that our current plight is widespread," Walter pointed out.

The four Squad members studied the crowd. One of the science teachers was tugging at her pants under the table, like she was trying to make them looser. And even their math teacher looked like she was in pain as she gingerly made her way across the cafeteria.

"Weird," Juan-Carlos agreed. After all, how did a whole school's underwear just disappear? And why?